MORE TALES OF THE CITY

Armistead Maupin

HARPER ● PERENNIAL

NEW YORK ● LONDON ● TORONTO ● SYDNEY

HARPER ● PERENNIAL

All photographs courtesy of Eric Liebowitz, Phil Bray, and Jean Demers for Showtime.

This work was published in somewhat different form in the *San Francisco Chronicle*.

Grateful acknowledgment is made for permission to reprint lines from "Shorts" from *Collected Shorter Poems, 1927–1957* by W. H. Auden. Reprinted by permission of Random House, Inc.

HarperCollins books may be purchased for educational, business, or sales promotional use. For information, please e-mail the Special Markets Department at SPsales@harpercollins.com.

First Perennial Library edition published 1980. Reissued 1989.
First Harper Perennial edition published 1994. Reissued 1998, 2007.

Designed by Cassandra J. Pappas

LIBRARY OF CONGRESS CARD CATALOG NUMBER 79-1710

ISBN: 978-0-06-092938-1 (pbk.)
ISBN-10: 0-06-092938-3 (pbk.)

17 18 19 LSCC 25 24 23 22 21